Little Duck's Missing Shirt

Fulton Books, Inc.
Meadville, PA

Published by Fulton Books 2021

ISBN 978-1-64952-867-4 (hardcover)
ISBN 978-1-64952-866-7 (digital)

Printed in the United States of America

Little Duck's Missing Shirt

RENAE JOHNS

One morning, Little Duck woke up and began to get ready for school.

He washed his face and brushed his teeth, just like Mommy Duck taught him.

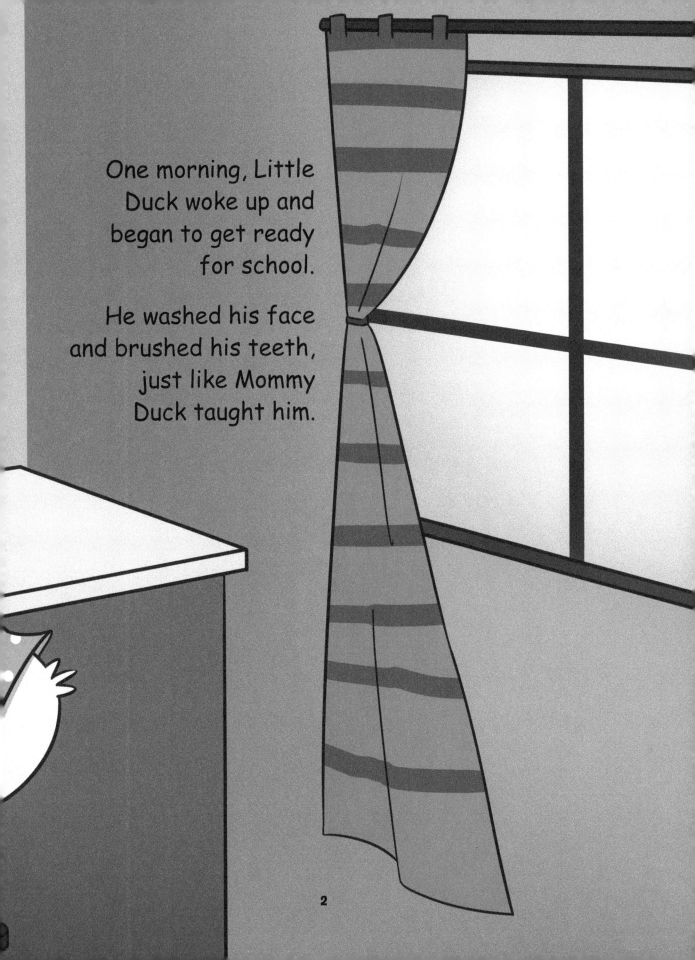

2

But when Little Duck went to get dressed, he could not find his favorite yellow shirt.

It was nowhere to be found!

He looked in his closet. No yellow shirt.

He looked in his dresser. No yellow shirt.

He asked Mommy Duck, "Have you seen my yellow shirt?"

Mommy Duck replied, "Little Duck, you need to get ready for school, or you will be late. Find a different shirt to wear."

Little Duck began to cry. "I need my yellow shirt!"

Mommy Duck asked, "Why Little Duck? Your green shirt is beautiful. Your red shirt is warm. Your blue shirt is brand new. What is wrong with those shirts?"

Little Duck replied, "Mommy Duck, everyone always wears a yellow shirt. I do not want to be different from everyone else!"

Mommy Duck suggested, "What if you wear a red shirt today? You could look like a beautiful ladybug sitting on a happy yellow flower when you stand next to your friends!

Or what if you wear a white shirt today? You would look like a fun polka dot on a comfy yellow summer blanket lying on the beach?

What if you wear a black shirt today so that you are the curious eye of a little bird as it sits in its tree and sings its happy song?"

13

Little Duck paused. "I don't know, Mommy Duck. It is so scary to be different than the other kids at school.

Big Bear always wears a yellow shirt. Cool Cat always wears a yellow shirt. And Zippy Zebra always wears a yellow shirt, and she is the smartest kid in the whole class!"

Mommy Duck told him, "I don't know, Little Duck. I think that it is a little boring to only see yellow shirts when we were given so many other beautiful colors of shirts to wear!"

Little Duck said, "Okay, today I will wear a green shirt. When I am with my friends, I will look like the one last green leaf on an autumn tree."

That day, he went to school wearing his green shirt.

When Little Duck got off the bus at the end of the day, h ran to Mommy Duck and cried, "Mommy Duck, it was oka that I wore my green shirt today!

Big Bear even told me that he *liked* it!"

Mommy Duck told him how proud she was and that he was brave for trying something new.

Little Duck was so happy that he decided to wear his green shirt the next day too.

18

When Little Duck went to school the next day, he wa[s] surprised! Big Bear was wearing a green shirt too!

Zippy Zebra was wearing an orange shirt! It looked so goo[d] with her black-and-white stripes!

Cool Cat was wearing a blue shirt that matched his eyes!

Even Mr. Owl was wearing a new red shirt that made hi[s] glasses look so cool!

19

Little Duck looked around and thought, *Wow, look at all the fun colors! They look so beautiful together!*

Mommy Duck was right. When everyone was wearing yellow shirts, they were all the same, but it was so boring! It was *much* more beautiful when all the colors came together. And no matter what color shirt they wore, they were all still friends!

"I am so glad that I was brave" said Little Duck. "I can't wait to wear my striped shirt tomorrow!"

About the Author

Renae Johns grew up in Western Pennsylvania where she still resides with her husband, children, and many pets. She holds a bachelor of science in mechanical engineering and a master's in business administration. Through her career, Renae has had the privilege of traveling all over the world, meeting people of different cultures, and learning to enjoy the beauty of diversity and differences. Instilling acceptance into her children was very important to Renae, so when the idea of *Little Duck's Missing Shirt* came to her, she had to share it with others as well.

CPSIA information can be obtained
at www.ICGtesting.com
Printed in the USA
LVHW070551140921
697767LV00009B/677